For Elizabeth and Suzanne Margulies
— T.S.

To Emelie and Louis
— G.F.

Copyright © 1996 by Scholastic Inc.
The activities on pages 27–32 copyright © 1996 by Marilyn Burns.

All rights reserved. Published by Scholastic Inc.
SCHOLASTIC, CARTWHEEL BOOKS, and associated logos
are trademarks and/or registered trademarks of Scholastic Inc.
Lexile is a registered trademark of MetaMetrics, Inc.

Library of Congress Cataloging-in-Publication Data is available.

ISBN-13: 978-0-590-22713-1
ISBN-10: 0-590-22713-0

16 15 14 13 12   11 12 13 14 /0

Printed in the U.S.A. 40 • This edition first printing, May 2008

Stay in Line

by Teddy Slater
Illustrated by Gioia Fiammenghi
Math Activities by Marilyn Burns

Cartwheel
B·O·O·K·S ®

SCHOLASTIC INC.
New York Toronto London Auckland Sydney
Mexico City New Delhi Hong Kong Buenos Aires

Twelve girls and boys
set off for the zoo.

Six pairs of children
lined up, two by two.

Everyone groaned
when the teacher said,
"Class, please stay in line.
Do not run ahead."

But staying together
turned out to be fun.
There were so many ways
that it could be done.

One dozen children
marched out the doors.
Three rows of children
marched out in fours.

Twelve boys and girls
climbed onto the bus

and sat three by three,
without any fuss.

At the zoo, all the children
skipped through the gate.

There was one line of four
and one line of eight.

Then twelve happy children,
each with a smile,
skipped toward the henhouse.
They skipped single file.

The whole class wanted
to look at the chicks.
So they crowded around them
in two rows of six.

At the llamas the children
could see for themselves
that the best way to stand
was in one row of twelve.

Later, the children
got down on their knees
to play with the bunnies
in twos and in threes.

Then all in a bunch,
the class fed the pigs lunch,
gave the ponies some oats,
and petted the goats.

By the time they had seen
every inch of the zoo,
there was only one thing
the kids wanted to do.

"You all must be tired," their teacher guessed. "Why don't you relax now and take a short rest?"

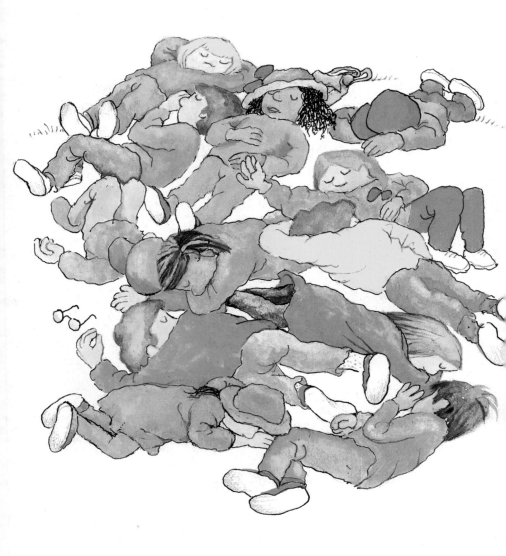

So twelve tired children
plopped down in a heap.
And, still all together,
they fell fast asleep.

• ABOUT THE ACTIVITIES •

If you look at one, two, three, four, or five objects, it's easy to see how many there are. However, more than five objects become a crowd. Counting one by one helps, and that's the only strategy young children have for determining amounts. But learning to organize larger quantities in different ways not only helps children see how many there are, but also helps them understand addition, subtraction, multiplication, and division.

In *Stay in Line!*, children see how one dozen children can be grouped in different ways. The activities and games in this section give children ways to become acquainted with the number 12 inside and out. While this section focuses just on the number 12, if your child is ready, expand to other numbers.

Working with physical materials helps make abstract mathematical ideas concrete. So collect twelve pennies and have them ready for your child to use. "Seeing" how to take apart a number and put it together in different ways helps children develop understanding. Be open to your child's interests and have fun exploring math.

— **Marilyn Burns**

You'll find tips and suggestions
for guiding the activities whenever
you see a box like this!

Hunting for One Dozen

Anytime you have twelve of something, you have a dozen. A full carton of twelve eggs is one dozen. Twelve cans of soda make one dozen. There were a dozen children going to the zoo.

Count things in your house. For each, guess first if you think there are exactly one dozen, more than one dozen, or less than one dozen. Then find out.

This activity gives children experience with estimating and verifying quantities. If your child is interested, suggest other objects to count as well. Also, if the word *dozen* is new for your child, this activity will help reinforce its meaning.

Are there a dozen chairs in your house?

How many forks? Exactly one dozen, more than one dozen, or less than one dozen?

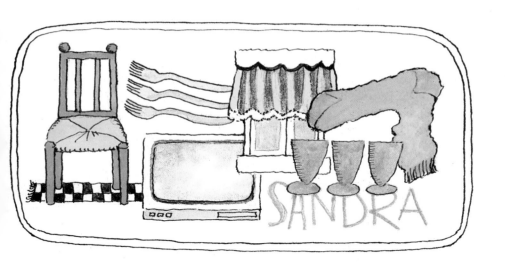

What about glasses in the cupboard?

Are there more or less than a dozen windows?

What about your socks? (If you had exactly one dozen socks, how many pairs would that make?)

Are there a dozen letters in your name? More or less? What if you count your first and last names?

Are there more or less than a dozen people with the same last name as yours in the phone book?

Do you have more or less than a dozen channels on your television?

What can you find exactly one dozen of?

Two by Two

At the beginning of the story, the children set off for the zoo in six pairs. Take twelve pennies and pretend each is one of the children. Use the pennies to show how the children lined up in twos.

Are there six pairs?

Can you count the pennies by twos? Try it — 2, 4, 6, 8, 10, 12.

Arranging pennies helps your child form visual images of the different ways 12 can be grouped.

Out the Door in Fours

When the children marched out the door, three rows of children marched out in fours. Use the pennies to show how the children marched.

Can you count the pennies by fours? Try it — 4, 8, 12.

Count them some other way to be sure there are twelve.

Your child may count them by ones, twos, or some other way. Any way that makes sense is fine.

On the Bus in Threes

Next the children got on the bus and sat in threes. Arrange the twelve pennies into threes, just like the children sat on the bus.

How many seats did the children fill?

Can you count the pennies by threes? Try it — 3, 6, 9, 12.

Count them some other way to be sure there are twelve.

Show the Other Ways

Arrange the pennies to show the other ways the dozen children stayed together.

They went through the gate in a line of four and a line of eight.

They skipped toward the henhouse in single file.

They looked at the chicks in two rows of six.

Then they lined up in one row of twelve.

They played with the bunnies in twos and threes.

All in a heap, they fell fast asleep.

How else could the dozen children have stayed together? Use your pennies to show other ways.

> If your child is interested, start with other numbers of pennies and explore what happens when you put them into different size groups. Point out when there are leftovers — such as when you put nine pennies into pairs.

What About Six?

Suppose only six children went to the zoo. If they lined up in twos, how many pairs would there be? Use six pennies to figure this out.

What if they sat on the bus in threes? How many seats would they fill?